10 Trick-or-Treaters

10 Trick-or-Treaters

A Halloween Counting Book

by Janet Schulman • illustrated by Linda Davick

Dragonfly Books

New York

10 trick-or-treaters
on a dark and spooky night
out to get some candy
or give someone a fright.

10 trick-or-treaters . . .

standing in a line.
Along came a spider . . .

and then there were 9.

9 trick-or-treaters,
the night was getting late.
A toad hopped near . . .

and then there were 8.

8 trick-or-treaters
under racing clouds in heaven.
A bat flew by . . .

and then there were 7.

7 trick-or-treaters
filling sacks with party mix.
A ghost said,
"Boo!" . . .

and then there were 6.

6 trick-or-treaters
dancing to some jive.
A skeleton tried
to join them . . .

and then there were 5.

5 trick-or-treaters knocking on a door. "Who's there?" called a witch . . .

and then there were 4.

4 trick-or-treaters
counting candy by a tree.
A monster cried,
"Gimme some!" . . .

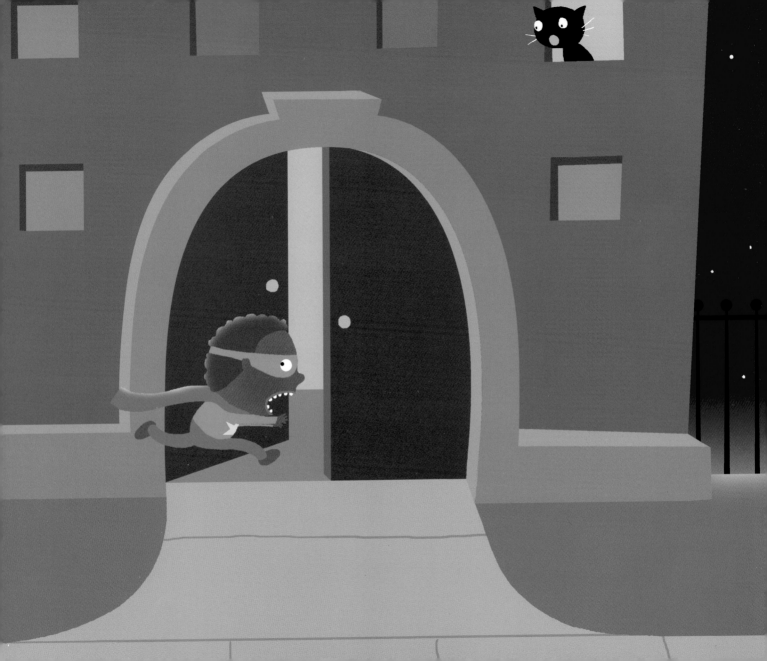

and then there were 3.

3 trick-or-treaters—
why are there so few?
A vampire crooned,
"Good evening" . . .

and then there were 2.

2 trick-or-treaters,
they've had a night of fun.
A mummy stumbled by them . . .

and then there was 1.

1 brave trick-or-treater,
her Halloween is done.
She climbed into bed . . .

and then
there were
none.

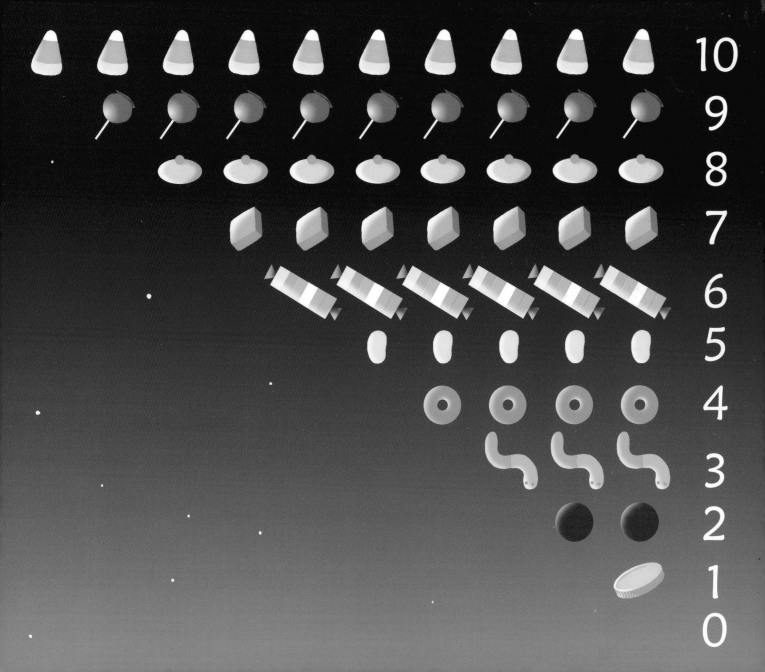

10

9

8

7

6

5

4

3

2

1

0

For Erin Clarke
—J.S.

For Princess Aggles
—L.D.

Published by Dragonfly Books
an imprint of Random House Children's Books
a division of Random House, Inc., New York

Text copyright © 2005 by Janet Schulman
Illustrations copyright © 2005 by Linda Davick

Visit us on the Web! www.randomhouse.com/kids
Educators and librarians, for a variety of teaching tools, visit us at www.randomhouse.com/teachers

The Library of Congress has cataloged the hardcover edition of this book as follows:
10 trick-or-treaters : a Halloween counting book / by Janet Schulman ; illustrated by Linda Davick.
Summary: Ten trick-or-treaters start out on Halloween night, but they disappear one by one as they encounter a spider,
a vampire, a ghost, and other scary creatures.
ISBN 978-0-375-83225-3 (trade) — ISBN 978-0-375-93225-0 (lib. bdg.)
[1. Halloween—Fiction. 2. Counting. 3. Stories in rhyme.] I. Title: Ten trick-or-treaters. II. Davick, Linda, ill. III. Title.
PZ8.3.S29737Aae 2005
[E]—dc22
2004010831

ISBN 978-0-385-73614-5 (pbk.)

Reprinted by arrangement with Alfred A. Knopf Books for Young Readers

MANUFACTURED IN MALAYSIA

First Dragonfly Books Edition
July 2008
10 9 8 7 6 5 4 3 2 1

Janet Schulman has worked in publishing for over forty years. She is the anthologist of *The 20th-Century Children's Book Treasury* and *You Read to Me & I'll Read to You* and the author of *Countdown to Spring!*, *A Bunny for All Seasons*, and *Pale Male: Citizen Hawk of New York City*. Janet Schulman is a resident of New York City, and her favorite Halloween candy is Good & Plenty.

Linda Davick is also the illustrator of *Kindergarten Countdown* by Anna Jane Hays. She lives and works near the ocean in San Francisco with her husband and Mabel the cat. Linda's favorite pastimes include expanding her sea-glass collection, eating take-out food, and drawing and eating candy at the same time.